THE SECRET SEVEN
SHORT STORY COLLECTION

THE SECRET SEVEN
SHORT STORY COLLECTION

by
ENID BLYTON

Illustrated by
Max Schindler

Hodder
Children's
Books

a division of Hodder Headline

This collection first published in Great Britain in 1997
by Hodder Children's Books
This paperback edition published 1997

For further information on Enid Blyton
please contact www.blyton.com

10 9 8 7 6 5

A Catalogue record for this book is available from the
British Library

ISBN 0-340-70934-0

Typeset by Hewer Text Composition Services, Edinburgh
Printed and bound in Great Britain by
Clays Ltd, St Ives plc

Hodder Children's Books
a division of Hodder Headline
338 Euston Road
London NW1 3BH

CONTENTS

The Secret of Old Mill

CHAPTER ONE
Peter has an idea

PETER WAS reading a book. He was sitting under a bush, almost hidden, and he hadn't said a word for over an hour.

'Peter!' said Janet. 'Peter! Do talk to me.'

Peter took no notice of his sister at all. He just went on reading. Then Scamper, the golden spaniel, pushed himself close to Peter and licked his nose.

Peter took no notice of Scamper either. Janet got cross.

'PETER! I keep talking to you and you don't answer. You're mean.'

Peter turned over a page, and was lost in his story again. Janet wondered what he could be reading. It must be a very very interesting book! She crawled under the bush beside him.

She looked at the title of the book, printed at the top of the left-hand page: 'The Secret Society.' Well, it sounded exciting. Janet felt as if she must read it, too! She leaned over Peter's shoulder and began to read as well. But he didn't like that.

'Don't,' he said, and pushed his sister away. 'You

know I hate people reading the same thing as I am reading.'

Then a bell rang in the distance.

'Bother!' said Peter. 'Now I'll have to stop. Janet, this is a lovely book; really, it is.'

He got up, and Janet got up, too. 'Tell me about it,' said Janet, as they went up to the farm-house for tea.

'It's about a Secret Society,' said Peter. 'There's a band of men who have a secret meeting-place and a secret password they use to let one another know they're friends. And they plan all kinds of things together.'

'Oooh, how lovely!' said Janet. 'I shall like reading that book. It's the one Granny gave you, isn't it?'

'Yes,' said Peter. Then he suddenly stopped, his face glowing with excitement. 'Janet! Why shouldn't *we* have a Secret Society, too – a secret band of boys and girls – and a secret meeting-place?'

'With a secret password,' said Janet, standing still, too. 'Peter – that would be marvellous!'

'Where could we meet?' wondered Peter. 'We'd have to plan all that. Oh, I know! Up at the tumbledown Old Mill!'

The tea-bell rang again, more loudly and impatiently. 'Mummy's getting cross,' said Janet. 'We'd better hurry. We can talk about it after tea. Oh, Peter – what a lovely idea!'

They went in to tea with Scamper at their heels. They were so excited that they almost forgot to go and wash their hands first. But Mummy soon reminded them!

They hardly said a word at teatime, because they were both so busy making their plans. Mummy felt quite worried.

'What's the matter with you both? You hardly say a word!' she said. 'Have you quarrelled?'

'Oh, *no*,' said Peter. 'Of course not. We've thought of a lovely plan, that's all.'

'Well, so long as it doesn't mean you getting too dirty, and so long as it's nothing dangerous, that's all right,' said Mummy. 'What is it?'

Peter and Janet looked at one another.

'Well,' said Peter, at last, 'it's a secret really, Mummy.'

'Then, of course, I won't ask any questions,' said Mummy at once. That was always so nice of her – she never made the children tell her anything if they didn't want to.

'I expect we'll tell you sometime,' said Peter. 'But we don't really know enough of the secret ourselves yet. I've finished my tea, Mummy. Can I go?'

He and Janet and Scamper rushed out of the old farmhouse, which was their home. It was called Old Mill Farm because of the tumbledown mill on the hill nearby, which had once belonged to the farm. It had been a famous mill in its day, and its great vanes had swung round thousands of times in the wind, to work the machinery that ground the corn for the farmer. It stood up on the sunny hill, its vanes broken and still now. The farmer no longer ground his corn there. It was an empty, dark old place, full of mice, owls, and spiders.

'Shall we go to the mill and talk over our plan?' said Janet. 'Nobody will hear us then.'

So off they went to the mill. They went in at the crooked old door, and found themselves in darkness, except for a few thin rays that crept in at cracks in the wall. The children didn't mind the quietness and the dark – they liked the old mill very much. They sat down in a corner.

'We'll talk in a low voice, because it's very, very secret,' said Peter. 'Now – who shall we have for our band, our Secret Society, Janet? Only boys and girls we really like and trust. We mustn't have anyone who will give the password away.'

'I should have Colin – and Jack – and Pam – and George,' said Janet. 'We both like them – and we know they can keep a secret, because we've tried them before. Let's get them all here on Saturday and have our first Secret Society meeting!'

'Yes – and choose the password, and plan what we are going to do!' said Peter. 'It *will* be fun! Let's have Barbara, too. I like her – she's good fun.'

'Right,' said Janet. 'Well, that's the first thing done – we've chosen the members of our Secret Society. Oh, isn't it going to be exciting, Peter!'

CHAPTER TWO
The first meeting

COLIN, PAM, Jack, George and Barbara, each had a strange message the next day. This is what they got: –

'Please come to the Old Mill at five o'clock on Saturday evening. Say nothing to anyone! VERY SECRET!'

The five children were puzzled and excited. They didn't say a word to anyone. As Janet had said, they could all be trusted to keep a secret.

Peter and Janet were at the Old Mill at half-past four, waiting. At ten to five Colin came. Two minutes later George and Jack arrived together. Then Barbara and Pam came exactly at five o'clock. They crouched down in the darkness, wondering why they had been told to come.

Peter suddenly spoke from a dark corner and made them all jump, because nobody knew that he and Janet were there.

'Hallo, everyone!' said Peter.

'Why – that's Peter's voice,' said Jack, and switched on a torch he had brought with him. Then they all saw one another.

'Why did you get us all here like this?' asked Jack. 'Is it a trick or something?'

'No,' said Peter. 'It's just an idea Janet and I had. We want to form a Secret Society of just a few boys and girls. With a secret meeting-place and secret password, you know.'

'And we chose you five because we like you, and we know we can trust you all to keep a secret,' said Janet.

'It sounds fine,' said George. 'What shall we have for a secret password?'

'Everyone must think hard,' said Peter. 'It's a word we must always say in a very low voice when we meet one another – or if we want to send a secret message, we must put the word in the message. And when we have secret meetings no one will be allowed in unless they first say the password.'

'What about Mississippi? Or some word like that?' said Barbara.

'Yes – or pomegranate, or some other unusual word?' said George.

'We might forget an ordinary word,' said Colin. 'We wouldn't forget one like pomegranate.'

'It's too difficult,' said Peter. So they all thought again. Then Pam spoke. 'What about something out of a nursery rhyme – Handy-Spandy – or Humpty Dumpty?'

'Or a game – tiddly-winks!' said Colin. 'I always like that name.'

Everyone liked the sound of tiddly-winks, and so they chose that for their secret password.

'The secret meeting-place will be easy,' said Janet. 'It can be here, in the dark old mill. Nobody ever comes here. We wouldn't be disturbed at all.'

'Couldn't we go up high in the old mill?' said Pam. 'There used to be an old stairway, or steps, or something, that led to a little room behind the middle of the vanes. I remember your father telling me about it once when I came to tea, Peter.'

'Well, the stairs are awfully broken now,' said Peter, getting up. 'But I dare say we could manage to climb up all right. It would be fun to go into that tiny room behind the vanes. If we wanted to keep things there, they would be quite safe.'

'Yes, we could bring food here – make it a proper Society Head-quarters,' said Colin. 'We might even meet here once in the middle of the night!'

'Gracious! I wouldn't dare to do that,' said Pam.

Everyone felt excited. They got up and looked for the old stairway. It was a good thing Jack had a torch with him, because there really wasn't enough light to see properly.

Some of the steps were missing. Some were half-broken. It was quite exciting to get up them into a dusty, cobwebby barn-like room above. This wasn't the little room Pam meant. Peter knew which that was. He took Jack's torch and shone it on to a small, narrow, spiral stairway in one corner. This led up to the tiny room behind the vanes.

This stairway wasn't as tumbledown as the one downstairs. The seven children climbed up one behind another. Peter stood still at the top barring the way.

'Secret Society Headquarters,' he said. 'Give me the password, please – in a whisper!'

'Tiddly-winks!' whispered Jack. 'Tiddly-winks,' whispered Pam, and they were let in. The others all remembered the password too, and were soon sitting down in a ring on the dirty floor.

'This is a very nice secret place,' said Jack. 'Peter, what's our society called? Have you thought of a name? What shall we be?'

'We'll be the Seven Society,' said Peter. 'There are just seven of us.'

'Yes! And Pam and Barbara and I will make tiny buttons with S.S. on,' said Janet. 'One for each of us!'

Everyone thought that was a fine idea. 'You must all promise most solemnly to keep our Seven Society a dead secret,' said Peter. And one by one they took his hand and promised very solemnly and earnestly.

'Usually a Society has a plan for something,' said Janet. 'Something to work for, I mean. What shall we plan?'

'Well, I've got an idea – though I don't know if you'll think it's a good one,' said Barbara, sounding rather shy. 'You know that little boy in the village? Well, he's got to have a big operation but he's got to go abroad to have it.'

'And we can help raise the money somehow for the trip!' cried Janet. 'That's what you mean, isn't it, Barbara? I heard Mummy say his poor old Granny couldn't afford to send him away. I think that's a fine idea for our Secret Society! I do, really!'

'Well – it would have been nice to plan something more exciting,' said Colin. 'But we can have another plan later. Are we all agreed? Yes, we are!'

CHAPTER THREE
The Secret Seven Society

AND SO the Seven Society was formed – with Peter for its chief, and Colin, George, Jack, Janet, Pam, and Barbara for the other members.

The girls set to work that very evening, as soon as they got home, to make the little badges. Janet begged three small buttons from her mother, and a bit of cloth. She covered each button in red, and then threaded a needle with bright green silk.

She neatly sewed S.S. on each button in green. They really looked beautiful when they were finished. Janet wondered if the other girls were making theirs as nicely as she had made hers.

She had made one for herself, one for Peter, and one for Colin. Pam was making Jack's and her own, and Barbara was making George's and her own. They had to be worn on Monday.

Peter and Janet pinned on theirs on Saturday night to see how they looked. 'You've made them beautifully,' said Peter, pleased. 'I feel very important wearing a button like this, with a secret sign on. Do you remember the password, Janet?'

'Skittles,' said Janet. Peter looked at her in horror.

'*Janet!* You've forgotten the password already. I'm ashamed of you, really I am. Skittles wasn't the word we chose. Think again.'

'Er – was it Musical Chairs?' said Janet, screwing up her face as if she was trying hard to think. Peter groaned.

'Oh, Janet – to think *you* should have forgotten it! I don't think I ought to tell you, either. You will have to confess your bad memory to the others and let them see if you can still belong.'

'Is it Hop-scotch – or Tip-and-run?' said Janet, giggling. Peter gave her a little punch.

'You're a bad girl! You do remember really! You're only making fun. Go on – what's the password?'

'Wuffy-wuff,' said Scamper suddenly. He had been listening to all this with his head on one side.

'Oh – didn't it sound exactly as if he wuffed out Tiddly-winks!' said Janet. 'Good old Scamper – you remembered the password, didn't you? Of course, I remembered it, Peter. I was just being funny.'

Peter was very relieved. He took off his button and hid it away. He would wear it on Monday, when all the others did. He stroked Scamper's smooth silky head.

'We didn't make you a member, did we?' he said. 'But you remembered the password all right, Scamper. What was it, now?'

'Wuffy-wuff,' said Scamper again, and Peter and Janet laughed and laughed.

All the Society wore their S.S. buttons on Monday morning. The other children in the class were puzzled and rather jealous. They all wanted buttons, too, but they didn't know what they were for.

'Sorry,' said Peter. 'It's a secret. Can't tell anyone, I'm afraid.'

The Society met on Monday evening again, at the Old Mill. They had all quite decided this should be their meeting-place. Janet and Peter were up in the tiny room before the others came. It had been arranged that as soon as the rest came, they were to stand at the bottom of the broken stairway and say the password. Then Peter would say: 'Pass, brother, and come up the stairs.'

Colin came in. He stood at the bottom of the stair-case, whilst Peter, in the little room far above, put his head out and listened. He heard Colin's voice down below.

'Tiddly-winks!'

Peter grinned to himself. 'Pass, brother, and come up the stairs!' he called, and up came Colin.

Everyone arrived, said the password, and was allowed to go up into the little room. There they made more plans.

'We shall need quite a lot of money to send little Luke away,' said Janet. 'I was asking Mummy how much we would need to raise, and she said at least seventy pounds to make a difference.'

Colin whistled. 'Seventy pounds! That's a lot of money – and even then it would only be a start.'

'Yes. But it's better than nothing,' said Janet. 'And if all seven of us work hard at something, surely we could earn ten pounds each by the end of term.'

'I'm going to earn my ten pounds helping with the hay-making,' said George.

'And I'm going cherry-picking,' said Jack. 'I believe I could earn more than ten pounds if I go each evening.'

They each had some kind of plan. They sat and talked eagerly up in the little dark room. It was really rather uncomfortable there, and when Janet had been sitting on the hard floor for a time, she had a good idea.

'Let's make this a *proper* headquarters,' she said. 'With a rug or two to sit on – and let's clean the place up a bit – and get a lamp or something to light it.'

'Oooh, yes – and a box for a table,' said Jack. 'And we'll bring a money-box here and drop our earnings into it at every meeting.'

'I like all these plans,' said Pam. 'I'll bring a brush and a pan – I've got small ones of my own.'

'And I'll bring an old rug out of our shed at home,' said Barbara. 'Nobody uses it but me. Mummy gave it to me last year.'

'Meet here on Wednesday evening,' commanded Peter, 'with anything likely to make our headquarters really comfortable. And if anyone can bring any food or drink, they can. We could have supper here one night then. It would be fun!'

'The Seven Society is *great* fun!' said Colin – and everyone agreed. But it was going to be even more exciting soon!

CHAPTER FOUR
A very surprising thing

THE NEXT time the Secret Society met, its members were very busy indeed! Pam brought a brush and pan. Barbara brought her old rug, and a broom to help in the cleaning. Janet brought a stool.

Jack brought a lantern that the gardener had lent him. It was filled with oil, and he had to be very careful when he lit it.

'I've got to put it in a very safe, steady place,' he said. 'The gardener said we mustn't play the fool and knock it over, or we'd go up in smoke.'

'Well, we don't behave stupidly,' said Peter. 'I'm your chief, and I chose you all because you're sensible people. I wouldn't have chosen Gordon, because he's always messing about, being silly – and he'd have knocked over the lamp at once!'

The lamp certainly made a difference to the Old Mill room. It lighted up all its dark corners, and made everything look very cheerful.

The children set to work to clean the little room. The dust was thick and made them choke as it rose into the air.

'Oh, dear – I suppose it will all settle again as soon as we've finished!' said Janet. 'Well, I've swept quite a lot into this corner, anyway!'

When the seven had finished the job, they put down the old rug that Barbara had brought. It made a very nice carpet in the centre of the little room. Then Janet's stool was set down, and a box that Colin had found down on the ground floor of the mill.

'That's our table,' said Peter. 'Anyone brought anything for a meal?'

'I've got some cakes that Mummy gave me,' said Pam. 'And Jack's got a whole bag of cherries. He's allowed to have as many as he likes when he goes cherry-picking.'

'And I've got some tarts Mummy made,' said Barbara.

The things were put on the table. 'It's a pity we haven't

any spoons and forks, and plates,' said Janet. 'Mummy wouldn't let me bring any of those. I did ask her.'

Jack rapped on the box-table. 'Spirit of the Old Mill, we want spoons and forks and cups!' he said, loudly. Everyone laughed. They began to eat the food hungrily. They wished they had thought of bringing something to drink.

'We'd better have a kind of store-cupboard somewhere here,' said Jack. 'Then if any of us comes here by himself, and is terribly hungry, he can help himself.'

'Does that mean you're going to visit the Old Mill each day?' said Colin, who knew what a big appetite Jack had. 'If you are, *I'm* not leaving anything behind!'

'Has everyone finished?' asked Peter. 'Because, if so, we ought to put our earnings into the money-box I've brought, and count it up.'

'Yes, we'll do that,' said Janet, and she put an old money-box on the table. It belonged to Peter and was in the shape of a pig. There was a slit in his back for the money. Underneath was a little place to unlock his tummy and take out the money. Peter had the key to that.

'How much is in the pig?' asked Colin, as each of them put in his bit. Peter was counting as it all went in.

'Goodness – we've put in fifteen pounds and forty pence already!' he said. 'I think that's really marvellous!'

'Have we, really?' said Janet, pleased. 'We'll soon have thirty pounds, then, and probably more by the time the term has ended. I think we're a very very good Secret Society!'

It really was fun to have a Secret Society, with a secret name and badges, and a password. Sometimes, when one of the members met another, they whispered the password just to enjoy feeling they belonged to the Society.

'Tiddly-winks!'

'Pass, brother!'

It was not long before the Seven Society had a nice little larder up in the tiny room. Into it was packed a whole lot of things – tins of condensed milk, packets of jelly cubes, jars of potted meat, biscuits and bars of chocolate. Bottles of ginger-beer were also put away in the dark corners, ready to be brought out at a Seven Society feast.

It was difficult to eat the condensed milk without a spoon, but nobody's mother would allow knives, forks, spoons, or crockery to be taken out of the children's homes. So they had to take it in turns to dip in their fingers and lick them.

'It's really disgusting, of course, eating it like this,' said Barbara. 'I do wish we had spoons and things.'

'I can't think what the spirit of the Old Mill is doing!' said Jack, with a grin. 'I told him to provide us with spoons and forks and cups the other day – and not a thing has he produced!'

'You're an idiot, Jack,' said Janet. 'Have you all finished? If so, I'll clear away. I'll put the things on this funny old shelf here – not on the floor. They won't get so dusty.'

She stood on tip-toe to put the things away on the high shelf. As she was pushing a tin to the back, it bumped into something. Janet got the stool and stood on it. She saw a bag at the back of the shelf, and she pulled it out.

'Who put this bag here?' she asked. She shook it, and it clinked.

Nobody seemed to have put the bag there. So Janet climbed down from the stool and opened it. She shook out the things that were in it.

Down they fell on the rug – forks and spoons by the dozen!

Everyone stared in astonishment. 'Spoons – and forks!' said Barbara, in a rather shaky voice. 'Oh, goodness, Jack – the spirit of the Old Mill must have taken you at your word – and sent you the spoons and forks you commanded!'

Well, what an extraordinary thing! But there were the spoons and forks, shining on the rug – it was all perfectly true and real!

CHAPTER FIVE
Eleven o'clock at night

BARBARA AND Pam were rather frightened.

It seemed such a strange thing to happen. As for Jack, he just made a joke of it.

'Thanks, old spirit of the Mill!' he said, and took up a spoon. 'Very nice of you. What about a few cups now to drink ginger-beer in? I did ask for some, you know.'

'Oh, don't!' said Pam. 'I'd just hate some cups to come from nowhere.'

'I'll see if there are any put ready for us on the shelf where Janet got these from,' said Jack, and he stood on the stool and felt about at the back of the rather deep shelf.

And he felt something there! Something very heavy indeed – a sack full of things that clinked.

Jack pulled it off the shelf. It was so heavy that when it fell to the ground he was almost pulled off the stool. Everyone stared in scared amazement. What next?

'Oh – I hope it's not cups,' whispered Barbara. 'I'd hate it to be cups.'

Without saying a word, Jack undid the rope that tied the neck of the sack. He put in his hand – and brought

25

out a silver cup! And another and another – all gleaming and shining brightly.

'Well – they *are* cups!' he said. 'Sports cups, it is true – but, still, cups. What shall we ask for next? Teapots or something?'

'You're not to talk like that,' said Janet. 'It's making me feel strange. Peter – what do you think is the meaning of this?'

'Well,' said Peter, 'it's nothing to do with Jack's silly commands, of course. I think that some thieves are using this old mill for a hidey-hole for their stolen goods.'

There was a silence. 'Do you really?' said George. 'Well, I hope they don't come whilst we're here!'

'Shouldn't let them up!' said Peter, at once. 'They wouldn't know the right password!'

'Idiot!' said Jack. 'They'd come up just the same.'

'I know what we'll do,' said Colin. 'We four boys will come along here late at night and watch to see who the thieves are. That would be a real adventure!'

'Yes!' cried Jack, George, and Peter at once. The girls were only too glad to be left out of this idea.

'We ought to tell somebody,' said Janet.

'Wait till we find out who the thieves are,' said Peter. 'Then we can go straight along to the police-station and tell our great news.'

The other boys were all for going to the Old Mill at eleven o'clock that night, and hiding to watch for the thieves. They felt sure they would be along to fetch their hidden goods. Janet was certain the sacks hadn't been there when she and the girls had cleaned the tiny room. So the thieves must have been along only a little time ago, and would, no doubt, come to get their goods at the first chance.

'There's no moon tonight, so it would be a good night for them to come,' said Jack. 'Well, boys – meet here at eleven. Give the password at the bottom of the stairs, and go up when you hear "Pass, brother," as usual.'

They all went home, excited. What an adventure that night for the boys!

At eleven o'clock, Peter was up in the tiny room in pitch darkness. A rat scuttled across the floor and made him jump. He waited for the others, wishing they would come.

Ah – that was somebody. It sounded like old Colin, blundering in. Peter was just about to call out to him when he stopped himself. Of course – he must wait for the password! What was he thinking of, not to wait for the password?

He waited. No password came. But somebody was coming up the broken stairs. In a panic, Peter stood up quietly in the tiny room far above. Soon whoever it was would be in the room beside him – he would be found by the thieves!

It *couldn't* be one of the Seven, because he hadn't heard any password. Silently, Peter made for a corner, and pushed himself behind a great beam he knew was there, though he couldn't see it.

A man came up the spiral stairway and into the tiny room. He switched on a torch and went to the shelf. He ran his torch over the shelf and then gave an angry grunt.

'Gone! The sacks are gone! That pest of a Lennie has been here first. I'll teach him he can't do things like that to me! Wait till I find him!'

Peter kept as still as a mouse whilst the angry voice was going on. Then his heart almost stopped beating. The light of the torch was shining steadily on the pig money-box! The thief had seen it.

He picked it up and shook it. When he heard the money inside, he dashed the pig to the floor and trod hard on it. The pig broke. The money came rolling out.

'Now, who put that pig up there?' said the man, and stooped to pick up the money. Peter could have cried to see all their hard-earned pounds and pennies going into the thief's pocket. But he simply didn't dare to say a word.

At last the man went. Peter hoped the other boys wouldn't run into him! They were very late. The sounds of stumbling down the broken stairs stopped, and there was silence again in the Old Mill.

After a bit, Peter crept out of his hiding-place. He was surprised to find that his knees were shaking. He almost jumped out of his skin when a word came up the stairs to him.

'Tiddly-winks!'

'Pass, brother,' said Peter, thankfully, and up came the other three boys – and behind them came Scamper the spaniel. Oh, how pleased Peter was to see them all!

CHAPTER SIX
What an adventure!

PETER TOLD them all that had happened. They listened without a word, most astonished – and were very upset when they heard that their savings had been stolen from the money-box.

'The girls *will* be miserable!' said Jack. 'I think we've made rather a mess of this, Peter. We ought to have told our parents, or the police, after all.'

'Yes. We ought,' said Peter. 'But I'll tell you what I think, boys – I think the second thief will be along soon, because I believe they were to meet here tonight and divide the stolen goods. This fellow thought Lennie, the other thief, had already been here and taken them. He didn't know we had hidden them safely away.'

'I see – and you think we might catch the second thief?' said Jack. 'Right. But I'm not risking anything now – one of us must go to the police-station and bring back the policeman!'

'All three of you can go,' said Peter. 'But I'll stay here and watch with Scamper. I'll be safe with him. Somebody must stay here and watch for the other thief, in case he comes before you get back.'

So the three boys set off again in the darkness, leaving Scamper cuddled against Peter's knees in the tiny room above. 'Now, you mustn't make a sound, see, Scamper?' said Peter. 'Ah – listen – what's that?'

It was a noise down below. Perhaps it was the boys coming back? Peter listened once more for the password. But it didn't come. So it must be the second thief. He tightened his hold on Scamper, who was longing to growl.

The thief came right up into the room. He, like the other man, went to the deep shelf and found nothing there. He swept his powerful torch round the room – and suddenly saw Peter's feet sticking out from behind the beam!

In a trice he pulled him out – but he let him go in a hurry when Scamper flew at him. He kicked at the dog, but Scamper wouldn't stop trying to bite him.

In the middle of all this a voice came up the stairs. The thief heard what it said in the greatest surprise. The voice said: 'Tiddly-winks,' very loudly indeed.

'*Tiddly-winks*,' said the thief, amazed. 'What does he mean, Tiddly-winks?' He went to the top of the spiral stairway and called down.

'Is that you, Jim Wilson? Have you taken the sacks? They're not here – but there's a boy and a dog here. Got to be careful of the dog!'

'Tiddly-winks!' yelled the voice again. It was Jack, anxious to know if Peter was all right.

'Pass, brother!' yelled back Peter. 'Look out – the other thief is here. Did you bring a policeman?'

'Two!' yelled back Jack. 'Nice big ones. Make the thief come on down. They're waiting for him.'

The thief was scared. He ran to some rickety steps in the corner of the room. They led up to a tiny attic at the very top of the mill. But Scamper was there before him, growling.

'That's right, Scamper! Send him down, send him down!' cried Peter. And Scamper obeyed. He worried at the thief's trousers, giving him nasty little nips in the leg till the man went stumbling down the spiral staircase. In the room below were the two policemen, waiting.

'All right. I'll come,' said the thief. 'Just call this dog off, will you? He's bitten my legs from ankle to knee, the little pest!'

'And what about your friend, who helped you to do the robbery?' asked one of the policemen, taking hold of the thief's arm. 'What about Jim Wilson?'

The thief had forgotten that he had called out Jim Wilson's name a few minutes before. He stared angrily at the big policeman.

'Oh, so you know about Jim Wilson, do you?' he said. 'Has he been telling tales of me? Well, I'll tell tales of *him* then!'

'Yes, go on,' said the policeman, and he took out a big black notebook to write down what the thief said.

'Jim Wilson's my mate and he lives at Laburnum Cottage,' said the thief. 'He and I did this job together, and we hid the stuff here. We meant to share it. But Jim's been here first and taken it. Yes, and hidden it somewhere safe, too, where *you'll* never find it!'

'But *we* know where it is!' cried Jack, and he swung his

torch round the room where they were all standing. 'Look – do you see that loose board there? Well, we put the spoons and forks and cups there, before we left here tonight! I think they're all solid silver. They feel so heavy.'

'Yes, they're silver all right,' said one of the policemen, pulling the sacks out of the hole under the board, and taking out a few of the things.

'The other thief took all our money out of the money-box,' said Peter, sadly. 'We'll never get that back, I suppose.'

'He'll have hidden it already, I'm afraid,' said the policeman. He snapped his black notebook shut. 'Well, come along, Lennie. We'll take you away safely and then go to Laburnum Cottage for Jim. Nice of you to tell us all about him.'

'You tricked me!' shouted Lennie. But his loud voice made Scamper growl again and fly at his trousers. 'Call this dog off!' he begged. Peter called him off. Scamper came back to him, still growling fiercely. Good old Scamper!

'What were you doing here, you boys?' said one of the policemen, as they left the Old Mill and went down the hill.

'Well – we four and three girls often come here,' said Peter. 'Sort of meeting-place, you know.'

'Oh – you've got a Secret Society, I suppose,' said the policeman. 'All children belong to one at some time or other. I did myself. Passwords and badges, and all that!'

'Yes,' said Peter, surprised that the policeman guessed so much.

'Tiddly-winks! Ho, that was a password, then?' said the first policeman, and he chuckled. 'I must say I wondered why you boys stood down there calling Tiddly-winks in the night! Well – your Secret Society did a lot of good, didn't it? It's caught us two thieves.'

'Yes. But it's lost us our precious savings,' said Peter. 'We worked hard for that money. We wanted it for Luke – to send him away on a holiday, you know.'

'Very nice idea,' said the policeman. 'I hope you get the money back – but I'm afraid you won't.'

They didn't. They were very sad about that when they met again the next day, being very careful indeed to use the password before climbing up the stairs.

The girls could hardly believe their ears when they heard about all the happenings of the night. They stared sadly at the battered, broken pig on the floor, and thought of all their hard work wasted.

But a day later something lovely happened. A letter came to Peter's house. It was addressed rather oddly: –

> THE CHIEF,
>   THE SECRET SOCIETY,
>   OLD MILL FARM.

'Well, look at that!' said Mummy. 'I suppose it's for you, Peter.'

It was, of course. Inside was a letter that made Peter and Janet squeal for joy.

'Dear Secret Society,
    I hear from the police that you helped them to catch the thieves who stole my silver, and that you hid it in safety when you found it. I am most grateful. Please accept one hundred pounds in gratitude for your Society's good work.
                    Yours sincerely,
                    Edward Henry White.'

'Gracious! That's the man the silver belonged to!' cried Peter. 'Mother, look! One hundred pounds! We can put it towards sending Luke abroad for his operation!'

Well, what a surprise! The two rushed off to tell the others the good news, and then off they all went to Luke. He could hardly believe his good luck.

The Secret Society of Seven is still going strong, and they still meet in the Old Mill. But Tiddly-winks is no longer their password, because too many people know it now.

They've thought of something else. It begins with an H and ends with a W, and I know it has something to do with a donkey.

Whatever can it be?

The Humbug Adventure

THE SECRET Seven met one day after morning school. 'What about this invitation from old Professor Wills to go and look at the planet Jupiter tonight through his telescope?' said Peter. 'I don't know why he's picked on *us* to ask!'

'I've already seen it on television,' said Colin. 'There wasn't much to see either!'

'It'll be awfully boring,' said Jack. 'He's not a bit interesting. He just drones on and on. Let's not go.'

'Well – wouldn't it be rude if we all left messages to say we weren't coming?' asked Janet. 'After all – he means it kindly. And he *has* got a jolly big telescope!'

'It's going to rain,' said Pam, looking up at the sky. 'I bet it is. So we shan't see a thing if we do go!'

'If it rains, we won't go,' said Peter. 'So we'll just hope that it pours and pours!'

It didn't. The sky was certainly cloudy, but no rain came at all. The Seven sighed as they ate their tea in their different homes. They would have to go after all!

So they went, waiting for each other outside Professor Wills's house, which was called 'Night Skies.' That made them laugh. At last each member was there, and in they went.

The maid showed them into a study, and then went to fetch the old professor. She came back looking sorry.

'It's such a cloudy night that the professor didn't expect you,' she said. 'So he's gone out. But his wife says that if you are very, very careful, she will show you how to work the telescope and you can see if you can spy Jupiter for yourselves. Ah – here she comes.'

Mrs Wills was very nice. To begin with she produced a tin of most enormous humbugs to suck. Then she showed Peter and the others how to train the big telescope on to different points of the sky. 'I know just about where the planet Jupiter is,' she said, 'and if you like I'll leave the telescope pointed at the place it should be, behind the

clouds. Then when the clouds move on you may catch a glimpse of it now and then.'

None of the Secret Seven could speak a word because of the big humbugs they were sucking. Peter made some polite noises, and hoped that Mrs Wills understood. When she had gone out of the room, the Seven looked at each other in relief.

'Ooogle, elescopy-oogle, urble, oopiter,' said Peter. Nobody understood. He put his eye to the end of the great tube and looked up.

'Uthing ooing,' he said, which the others correctly understood as 'Nothing doing.' Jack worked his humbug round to the other side of his mouth.

'Urgle, onky, ooky ky,' he said, meaning 'Let's not look at the sky,' but nobody understood a word! So he took his humbug out of his mouth and explained:

'Let's not bother about looking at the cloudy sky,' he said clearly. 'Let's bend the telescope down a bit and look at the village and the hills beyond and the farm – things like that. It would be fun to stand here, far away from them, and see them almost as if we could touch them!'

'Yes, let's,' said Peter. 'We know how to move the telescope. But for goodness' sake be careful, it's jolly valuable.'

The telescope had a curious window of its own to look through – a great window that reached from ceiling almost to ground, and had no glass in at all. It could be swung to almost any angle at a touch of the finger once a screw had been loosened.

'Let's look at the Village Hall,' said Janet. 'There's a dance on and it's all lit up.' She had taken her humbug out of her mouth to speak, and put it back again when she had finished. Peter was afraid of sticky finger-marks on the telescope, and he handed Colin a clean hanky to wipe where anyone touched.

The Village Hall looked so near that it might have been in the garden. Barbara took her sweet out of her mouth and giggled. 'There's Mrs Dickson, look, standing at the door. And do look, there's that silly boy Harry selling programmes or something.'

This was a marvellous game! They moved the telescope into another direction, and saw where a Fair was, in the farmer's field about a quarter of a mile away.

'Goodness – it looks so near that I'm sure I heard that

roundabout man sneeze!' said Janet. 'And I can even see Dickie and Danny, the twins, paying their pennies to go on together!'

They spent a long time looking at the Fair, and began to wish they were there. 'Urgle, ooble, oo,' said Peter, forgetting to take out his humbug, but the others knew what he meant, because he was swinging the telescope slowly to a different direction. It was now pointing towards the dark farm. One window was brilliantly lighted and no curtains were drawn.

'There's nice Mrs Wingfield knitting in her chair,' said Barbara, taking her turn.

'And old Mr Wingfield filling his pipe,' said Colin. 'I can even see what tobacco he's using!'

'You *can't*,' said everyone, mumbling through their humbugs. Then it was Jack's turn. He bent and looked through the great tube, seeing the farm itself and the barn nearby and a haystack. He suddenly gave a loud exclamation, and most unexpectedly swallowed his humbug. He gasped and choked, tried to call out something and pointed to the telescope. In astonishment, Peter looked through it. What was Jack fussing about?

He soon saw! Someone was moving near the haystack. Someone was striking matches! Little flames sprang up in the dry stack, and soon there were many more. Peter gasped, not taking any notice of poor, choking Jack. His eye was glued to the big telescope.

He squashed his humbug into his cheek in order to speak clearly. 'Fire! There's a tramp firing Farmer Wingfield's stack – and it's jolly near the old barn. Gosh, that's a big flame! Colin, go and ring up the

farmer – at once! And, after that, the police. Buck up, idiot! The stack will soon be burnt down, then the barn will catch!'

Colin ran to find the telephone in the hall. Peter had his eye glued to the telescope, watching everything. There was the man again, coming from behind the stack. He had probably fired the other side too! Peter could see him clearly – a small man – with a limp – and a beard that showed up well when he turned sideways to the flames. Janet tried to pull her brother away so that she could have a turn herself, but he wouldn't budge.

Colin telephoned to the farm and gave them a warning. Then he got on to the police. He ran back into the telescope room. 'Peter, I've phoned! What's happening now?'

Peter was having a most wonderful view of all the sudden excitement at the farm. The farm-door was flung open, and out ran the farmer and his son. His wife followed with buckets. A minute later the police came up in a car. Then firemen, called by the police, arrived too. What a to-do! Peter gasped and exclaimed, and the others could hardly contain themselves!

'Let's have a look, Peter! Peter, you selfish thing, let *us* have a turn. What's happening?'

Peter told them. 'Everyone's arrived – the stack's blazing, but the barn is safe. The firemen are drenching the stack now – and goodness, they've caught the man. No – it's not him. The man who fired the stack was small and had a beard and a limp. They've got the wrong man – no wonder he's struggling!'

This was too much for the others. They raced out of the room together. 'We're going to the farm! It's too thrilling for words!'

So down to the farm they went, and managed to see the end of the excitement. Half the stack was saved – the barn was not touched – and a man was trying to get away from two stout policemen.

'I didn't fire it, I tell you!' he was shouting. Jack went up to the Sergeant, who was standing nearby.

'Sir – I don't think that man did do it,' he said. 'The man you want has a limp – he's small – and has a beard.'

'Why – that would be Jamey!' cried the farmer's wife. 'We sent him off last week for stealing.'

The police let the other man go. The Sergeant ordered them to go to Jamey's cottage, not far off. Then he turned to Jack.

'Now perhaps you'll tell us how you know all this, you kids?' he said with his large smile. 'Warned the farmer – called the police – and even know who the man is who fired the stack! You're the Secret Seven, aren't you? Always into something, I know!'

'We saw it all through Professor Wills's telescope,' said Jack. 'Peter's still back there, watching.'

But he wasn't. As soon as he saw the others through the telescope, appearing in the midst of the excitement, he wanted to be with them – and he ran at top speed, sucking the very last of his humbug!

'Good work,' said the Sergeant, when Peter told the whole of the story. 'You saw something more exciting than the planet Jupiter, didn't you? Ah – you never know

47

what you're going to see through telescopes.'

'It was a jolly good adventure, but a very sudden and short one,' said Colin.

'Yes,' said Peter. 'It only lasted as long as my humbug. An adventure *couldn't* very well be shorter than that!'

'Short and sweet – like the humbug,' said Janet with a giggle. 'Let's call it the Humbug Adventure – it's a jolly good name for it!'

So it is – don't you agree?

Adventure on the Way Home

'WELL, IT's about time to go home,' said Peter, looking at his watch. 'I've still got some homework to do, too, worse luck. Come on, Janet. Thanks awfully for a jolly nice time, Colin.'

'Nice to have you all!' said Colin, as Peter and Janet and the rest of the Secret Seven went to the door. He had asked them all to tea on a dark winter's afternoon, and they had played card-games and a mad game of tiddly-winks, and had a jigsaw competition, which Janet won easily.

'Oooh – isn't it dark?' said Barbara, as they all stood on the front-door step. 'Not even a star to be seen. Anyone brought a torch?'

The boys had torches, and flashed them on as they walked down to the front gate. Colin shouted a last goodbye and shut the door. Scamper, the golden spaniel, ran ahead – he was always asked out to tea when the others were, of course.

The six children walked down the road and round the corner. 'Let's take the short-cut down by the canal,' said Peter. 'Then we can leave George at his house on the way.'

'I don't like that cut by the canal,' said Pam. 'It's so dark. Anything might happen!'

'Let it!' said Jack. 'Who minds if something happens! It would be fun. I wouldn't mind a spot of adventure this evening. I feel excited after all those games.'

'Well, adventures never come if you expect them,' said Janet, and walked straight into a dustbin that someone had left outside a door. Crash!

Janet yelled and three torches were shone on her at once. Jack picked up the dustbin lid, which Janet had knocked off, and Peter looked to see if his sister had hurt herself. She rubbed her right knee and groaned.

'I might have known that something silly would happen if I said that about adventures!' she said. 'Oooh, my knee! Why ever do people leave dustbins on the pavement?'

As they stood there, waiting for Janet to stop groaning, Scamper suddenly gave a growl. Peter shone his torch on to him.

'What's up, Scamper? Did the falling dustbin frighten you?'

Scamper was staring across the road, standing perfectly stiff, his tail down. The children looked across the road, too. What was Scamper so interested in?

A row of tall houses used for offices and small factories stood dark and silent in the cold winter's evening. Only one window showed a light, and that was not very bright because a ragged blind was pulled down over it. The light shone through the rents in the blind.

As the six stood there, they heard a scream and a little

cold shiver of fright ran over them. Scamper growled again, and the hair rose at the back of his neck, just as it did when he saw a dog he didn't like.

'Something's up,' said Peter uneasily. 'What shall we do? Listen – now there's somebody shouting!'

They all listened intently, their eyes fixed on the lighted window with the torn blind. A shadow suddenly passed across it, and Janet clutched Pam.

'Look! That was a man's shadow – and he had his hand up – he was going to hit someone. Oh, there's another scream. Peter, what shall we do?'

'I'll go and tell Colin – he ought to be in on this,' said Jack. 'I'll bring a rope, too. One of us can climb up to that window and see what's going on. I won't be a minute!'

In great excitement he shot off, back to Colin's house. Peter put his hand on the growling Scamper. 'Let's go and try the door of that house,' he said. 'It might be unlocked, you never know. It would be much easier to go in and up the stairs than to mess about with a rope.'

They crossed the road cautiously, switching off their torches. They came to a few steps that ran up to the front door of the house, and Peter went up to the door itself. He found a handle there and turned it.

But the door would not open. As he had expected, it was locked. He felt about for the letter-box, pushed it open and looked through it, flashing his torch there at the same time. But all he could see was a dark, rather dusty-looking hall, with boxes piled high on one side. The house was obviously used as offices and probably was a warehouse, too.

'Nothing to be seen,' said Peter, switching off his torch. 'My word – something *is* certainly going on up there. That was a most bloodcurdling howl just then!'

The five children on the doorstep felt most uncomfortable, and Barbara was scared. The shouts and cries sounded so fierce and the screams so helpless – and there were now loud thuds, too. Whatever *was* going on?

'I'm going for the police,' said Peter, making up his mind. 'You girls had better come with me. George, you stay here with Scamper.'

But Scamper would not stay with George. He wanted to go with Peter and Janet, of course. So, in the end, Peter ran off alone to get the police, and George and the three girls were left with Scamper to guard them.

Just round the corner Peter bumped into two running

boys – Colin and Jack. Colin, very excited, carried his mother's clothes-line, as that was the only rope he could think of. He clutched at Peter, recognizing him by the rather dim light of a nearby lamp-post.

'What's up, Peter? What's happened now? Why are you running away?' demanded Jack.

'I'm fetching the police,' said Peter. 'Something jolly serious is going on – and somebody's being hurt!'

He dashed off, and Colin and Jack ran to join the girls and George.

'Hallo!' he panted. 'I've brought a rope. Now we'll be able to see what's happening!'

They shone their torches upwards, and Jack pointed to a signboard swinging just below the lighted window.

'Throw the rope over the iron arm that holds the sign,' he said. 'Here – tie a stone to one end, and chuck it up. Then one of us can shin up easily.'

They tied a stone to the rope-end, and then Colin threw it deftly up to the signboard that was swinging in the wind. It fell neatly over it, and the heavy stone brought the other end of the rope down to the waiting children.

'Good – now we've got a double-rope to climb,' said Colin, pleased. He knotted the two ends together and twisted the double-strands so that Jack would have a good hold as he climbed up. 'There you are,' he said. 'Now you can shin up the rope just as you do at gym! I'll hold it steady so that it doesn't untwist.'

'Buck up, for goodness' sake!' said Pam, as another yell came from the room above. 'I can't bear this much longer!'

Jack shinned up the rope. He came to the signboard and pulled himself up by it to the strong iron bar that held it, jutting out from the brick wall under the lighted window. Cautiously he first sat, then stood on the bar, and found himself waist high with the window-ledge. He sat on the ledge and peered through a tear in the blind. What he saw made him slide down the rope at top speed, almost tearing his hands as he went.

'What is it? What did you see?' asked the others, crowding round.

'Whew!' said Jack, rubbing his hands gently. 'It's a good thing Peter's gone for the police. There are about nine people there, all going mad, as far as I can see. They've got awful faces, and they're yelling at one another and they've got knives, and two of them are lying on the floor, and a poor girl is kneeling down, crying for mercy, and . . .'

'My word!' said Colin, shocked, and the others gasped in horror, too. Scamper growled again and again, and then gave such an ENORMOUS growl that he made the children jump. They heard the sound of running feet, and held their breath. Who was this coming at top speed?

Ah – thank goodness, it was Peter and two burly policemen. Everyone heaved sighs of relief. Peter ran up, panting.

'Anything else happened? Quick, tell me!'

'I climbed up to that signboard and peeped in at the window through a hole in the blind,' said Jack. 'There's a terrible quarrel going on, and . . .'

The policemen listened as he gabbled out what he had seen. All was quiet in the room above now – not a shout was to be heard, not a scream, not a thud. Had the people there heard the arrival of the police?

'We'll go in,' said one of the policemen. 'Look, this bottom window's not fastened. Give me a leg-up, Joe.'

Both men went in – and, of course, the Secret Seven at once followed. They were not going to be left out of the fun! Besides, everyone felt quite different now that they had two stout, burly policemen with them! Scamper was left outside, and whined miserably.

Everyone crossed the office in which they found themselves, and went into the hall and up the stairs. The policemen had rubber-soled shoes and went quietly. The Seven, following some way behind, in case the two policemen saw them and sent them back, went quietly, too, their hearts beating fast. Really, what a very sudden adventure!

The police came to a door, under which showed a crack of light. They stood and listened. The seven came cautiously along, too, and stood on the landing, hoping that the policemen would not see them in the darkness.

A voice came sharply from inside the room. 'Now then – up you get! That's enough rest. Where's my knife? Scream, Margaret, and you, Hal, yell at her.'

Then the screaming and shouting began again, with pants and thuds. It seemed as if a terrific fight had begun all over again. The children clutched one another in fright.

One of the policemen flung open the door, and at once bright light streamed on to the landing. 'Now then – what's all this? What's going on here?' said the first policeman, standing in the doorway, gazing at the strange, startled faces turned towards him.

'Well! I *like* that! What are *you* doing here, I should like to know?' said a man's voice angrily. Peter saw that he held a knife in his hand. 'We've got permission to use this room – you ask the owner of this warehouse. We all work here.'

'Maybe. But what's all this fighting and quarrelling – and just you put that knife down, young man,' said the policeman, taking out a notebook and pencil.

A girl came forward with brilliant red cheeks, eyes made up in green and black, and an untidy mop of red hair which looked like a wig. She laughed.

'Did you think this was a *real* quarrel, a *real* fight?' she said. 'It's not! We're rehearsing a pirate play, and this is the fight scene, where I'm captured and a fight goes on between the pirates and my rescuers. I have to scream

like anything! We're giving the play tomorrow, that's why we're all dressed up and our faces are made-up with grease-paint!'

The two policemen were quite taken aback, and went off with many apologies. The Secret Seven scuttled downstairs in dismay. Goodness gracious! So it was just the rehearsal of an exciting play. *Now* they would get into trouble for fetching two policemen along for nothing!

But they didn't get into trouble. The policemen were very nice indeed about the whole thing. 'You did right to fetch us,' said one. 'It *might* have been something serious. You couldn't possibly tell. Now, you run home before you find any more adventures – or your next one will be your parents after you with a cane!'

Peter told his father and mother why he and Janet and Scamper were so late. They had been very anxious about them. Peter's father laughed when he heard of the evening's happenings.

'Well, well – you little idiots! Always wanting to put your noses into something! Shall I get tickets for the pirate show tomorrow evening – and take all the Secret Seven with me?'

'Oh, *yes*!' said Peter in delight. 'What a lovely end to an adventure that wasn't really an adventure. But, my word – it did *seem* like one, didn't it, Janet?'

'It did,' said Janet. 'But now everything's all right, and let's hope that *none* of the Secret Seven gets into a row.'

Nobody did except Colin – he had left his mother's clothes-line hanging over the swinging signboard! His mother won't let him go to the pirate play unless he fetches it back. It's all right, Colin – it's still there!

An Afternoon with the Secret Seven

THE SECRET Seven were having a meeting. The shed door was fast shut. A curtain was drawn across the little window in case Susie, Jack's sister, should make herself a nuisance and come peeping in, as she sometimes did.

The Seven were inside the shed, drinking lemonade given by Peter's mother and eating peppermints brought by Colin.

'This is rather a *dull* meeting,' said Barbara, bored. 'I thought we were going to plan something to do when you called the meeting, Peter – but we haven't planned *any*thing.'

'Well, nobody has any good ideas,' said Peter. 'It's not *my* fault if you're all brainless today.'

'Well, you're as brainless as the rest of us!' said George. 'I suppose it's because it's such a hot summer day – honestly, I'm melting in this shed.'

'Wuff,' said Scamper, the golden spaniel, as if he quite agreed. He lay on the floor, panting.

'He says he's worse off than we are because he has to wear a fur coat, and we're all in short-sleeved shirts or dresses,' said Jack with a grin.

'Listen – someone's coming!' said Janet suddenly. They listened and heard the tip-tap of footsteps coming down the path to the shed.

Then there came a knock at the door.

'Password!' yelled Peter at once.

'Sorry. I don't know it,' said a voice.

'Oh, Mother – I didn't know it was *you*,' said Peter. 'Have you come to bring us some more lemonade as you said you would?'

He opened the door, and there stood his mother with a big jug in her hand. She smiled at them all. 'Yes – here's the lemonade – with ice in it this time. My word, you do look hot! Haven't you finished your meeting yet?'

'Well, yes – I suppose we have,' said Peter. 'But we haven't settled much, I must say. We wanted to plan something exciting to do – but we can't think of *any*thing, Mother!'

'Well, how would you like to help me at the Garden Party in the vicarage garden this afternoon?' asked his mother. 'I could do with some sensible helpers like you.'

'Oh – I'd *like* to help,' said Barbara at once, and Pam nodded too. 'Garden parties are fun.'

'Will there be anything to eat?' asked George.

'I will buy you a nice tea there, and an ice each if you'd like to help,' said Peter's mother. 'The five Harris children were coming to help, but one of them has measles, so none of them can come. You'd do very well instead!'

'We'll come and help for *nothing*,' said Jack. 'My mother's going too – *she*'ll buy me my tea.'

'What do you want us to do?' asked Pam.

'All kinds of things,' said Peter's mother. 'But I'd *particularly* like you to help with the hoopla-stall and the coconut-shy next to it. The Harris children were going to run those themselves.'

'Oooh – it sounds fun,' said Colin. 'What time shall we be there, please?'

'At half-past two sharp,' said Peter's mother. 'Washed, brushed and tidy, please. I'll expect you all punctually!' And away she went back to the house.

'Well – we've got something exciting to do, after all!' said Peter, pleased. 'Pour out the lemonade, Janet – I just seem *never* to stop feeling thirsty in this weather – and let's get out of this hot shed now our meeting is ended.'

At half-past two all the members of the Secret Seven

were waiting in the vicarage garden, just by the hoopla-stall, Scamper as well. A tall lady came bustling up, smiling.

'Ah – you're the Secret Seven, aren't you?' she said. 'Peter's mother said you would be here. She's busy with the cutting of sandwiches for tea, and asked me to tell you what to do. Four of you are to manage the hoopla-stall – and three the coconut-shy. Now – do you know how to run them?'

'Yes, thank you, Mrs James,' said Janet. 'Peter and I have had a hoopla-stall before, and a coconut-shy is easy.'

'There's just one thing,' said Mrs James. 'You must be very careful with the money. You see, sometimes not very honest people come to garden sales, and if you should happen to leave your money-bag unattended for a few minutes, it might be stolen – and we do need every penny we can get this afternoon.'

'We'll be very careful, Mrs James,' said Peter. He turned to the others. 'Get busy now. Janet, Pam, George and I will manage the hoopla-stall – and you, Colin, can manage the coconut-shy with Barbara and Jack. One to take the money – one to set up the coconuts when they are knocked down – and one to give out the balls to throw at the coconuts.'

'Right,' said Colin, feeling important, and he and Jack began to set up the coconuts in their places.

Peter and Janet set out the things meant for the hoopla-stall. George tried the rings over each one to make sure that none was too big to be covered. Pam began to shout.

'Hoopla! Try your luck! Three rings for sixpence! Win a toy, or a bar of chocolate! Win a butter-dish or a little vase – or this pack of cards!'

People soon came up to the hoopla-stall and the coconut-shy. The Secret Seven worked very hard indeed, and even Scamper joined in, picking up any hoopla-rings that slithered off the stall after being thrown.

It was fun. Great fun! Pam shouted each time people came near, and Janet gave out the wooden rings and took the money. George and Peter watched the rings being thrown, gathered them up and gave them to Janet. When anyone threw a ring that fell completely round one of the things on the stall, Peter gave the article to the customer with a polite little bow.

'Congratulations!' he said. 'You have won this beautiful prize!'

The money was put into Peter's cap. He had forgotten to bring a bag of some kind, but his cap did just as well, Janet threw all the money she took into the cap, and carefully counted out any change necessary.

The three at the coconut-shy were doing well. Jack took the money and gave out the balls. He had no cap to put the money into, so he simply slid it into his shorts pocket each time – and that pocket soon began to feel very heavy!

'Only four people have won a coconut,' he told Peter, when he had a minute to spare. 'That's all! We still have plenty of coconuts left. I say – shall I put my money into your cap? I'm sure it will make a hole in my pocket soon, I've taken so much.'

'Yes, put it there,' said Peter. 'Look, you've got another customer. Buck up.'

Presently, about four o'clock, Peter's mother came up, smiling all over her face. 'I hear you Seven are doing very well,' she said. 'You do look hot, standing out here in the sun. What about some tea? And there are lovely ice-creams. Leave one of the Seven in charge of the stalls just for now, to see that no one comes along and makes off with a coconut or a hoopla prize. He can have his tea afterwards.'

'I'll stay,' said Peter. 'I'm head of the Seven. Go on, you others – I'll be in charge here. Scamper, you go, too.'

But Scamper wouldn't leave Peter. He stayed behind waiting for more hoopla-rings to pick up, but as most of the visitors were now having tea and ices, there were no customers at all.

Peter felt bored. He began to rearrange some of the hoopla things when someone called him. 'Hey, Peter! Come and have a ride on my pony! I've no customers just now, nor have you.'

It was Fred Hilton, who had brought his pony to the Garden Party and was taking quite a lot of money giving six-penny rides to children.

'Well – I'm really in charge of these two stalls,' said Peter, longing to ride the frisky little pony.

'Leave Scamper on guard,' said Fred. 'He'd never allow anyone to meddle with the stalls. Anyway, there's nobody about at all. Come on!'

'Right,' said Peter. 'Scamper – you're on guard, see? Look, I'll put my cap of money under the hoopla-stall – nobody must touch it, Scamper – or anything else either. Now, lie down – you're on guard.'

Scamper lay down, looking very important. He kept his eye on the cap of money. Peter went off happily with Fred. 'I'll give you a longer ride than anyone,' said Fred. 'All round this big garden three times!'

By the time Peter had gone round three times, the other members of the Secret Seven had finished their tea and had come back to the stall.

'Where's Peter?' said Barbara. 'Oh, there he is, look – just jumping off Fred's pony. Peter, Peter – you're to go and have your tea now – and there are *two* ice-creams waiting for you!'

Peter waved his hand and ran off to the tea-tent, calling his thanks to Fred. My – what a tea! All kinds of sandwiches, piles of little cakes, slices of creamy chocolate cake – and what ENORMOUS ice-creams!

Peter spent at least twenty minutes over his tea, and then went back to the hoopla-stall, feeling much better. Janet called to him as soon as he came.

'What did you do with the money, Peter? I wanted some change and I simply *couldn't* find your cap with the money in it.'

'It's under the hoop-la stall – you must be blind!' said Peter. 'I hid it there, and left Scamper on guard.'

'Well, it isn't there now,' said Janet, looking suddenly worried. 'I looked everywhere for it. Oh, Peter – and there was such a *lot* of money, too!'

Peter went to look under the stall at the back, where he had put his cap full of money. Certainly it was not there now. His heart sank. Why, oh why had he gone off to have a ride on Fred's pony! And where was Scamper? He had left him on guard.

'I expect Scamper went off somewhere, too,' said Colin. 'He saw you going off with a friend – and I bet he went off with someone, too – that little Scottie, I expect – he always loves to frisk about with him.'

'But – but there was *nobody* about, nobody near the stall at all!' said poor Peter, bewildered. 'I looked each time I rode past. I couldn't see Scamper, but I felt sure he was still lying beside my cap, where I had left him. Gosh – this is simply awful. Whatever are we to do?'

'You'd better tell your mother,' said Pam, looking rather white. 'Someone's robbed us – and it was such a lot of money. We were in charge, too – oh, *why* did you go off with Fred?'

Peter went to find his mother, feeling scared and upset. He thought crossly about Scamper. What did he *mean* by going off when he was on guard? He knew perfectly well what 'on guard' meant – and usually he never, never left the thing he was told to guard. But he must have left the cap of money or it would not have been stolen!

'Your mother's gone home for half an hour,' said Mrs James. 'Just to feed the hens, I think she said. She'll be back soon.'

Peter wondered what to do. Then he decided to go home and tell his mother before she came back. He would have a chance then to open his money-box and take out all the money there, to help to pay back what had been stolen.

He called to Janet as he passed the hoopla-stall. 'I'm going to slip home for a minute – and get my money-box – and tell Mother what's happened. She's gone back to feed the hens. Look after the stalls, all of you – and mind you scold Scamper well when he comes back, Janet.'

He ran all the way home, panting. Just outside the front gate he saw something shining on the path. It was a shilling!

'Well, *that's* a bit of luck!' said Peter, and picked it up. He opened the gate – and there, on the other side, was a six-pence! He picked that up, too, and went on to the door.

On the mat were two pennies! 'Most mysterious,' thought Peter. 'Perhaps Mother has a hole in her pocket and these dropped out!'

'Mother!' he called, opening the door. 'Mother! Are you here? I want to tell you something.'

Just as his mother called back to him, Peter heard a noise. 'Wuff, WUFF, WUFF!' It was Scamper's bark. Had Scamper run off home then, bored at being alone?

'Is Scamper home, Mother?' he said, running to find her.

'Yes – he's in his basket – and I don't think he can be very well!' said his mother. 'He growls every time I go near him! But why have you come back – you ought to be in charge of the hoopla-stall!'

'Mother – all the money we took is gone,' said Peter. 'I left Scamper guarding it under the hoopla-stall, while I went for a ride on Fred's pony – and when I got back the cap of money was gone!'

'Oh, *Peter!*' said his mother, shocked. 'How *could* you let such a thing happen!'

'Well, I left Scamper on guard,' said Peter. 'Scamper – where are you? My word, I do feel angry with you – letting me down like that!'

Scamper sat up in his basket. 'Come here,' said Peter sternly. Scamper put his head down and rummaged about in his rug. Then he leapt out of the basket and ran to Peter – and dropped something at his feet.

It was the capful of money! Scamper looked up at Peter and wagged his tail as if to say, 'Well, I guarded it, you see! I didn't know where you'd gone, so I took it home for you. It's quite safe!'

'Scamper! So *you've* got my cap of money!' said Peter, his heart suddenly much lighter. 'I suppose the money I found by the gate and by the door must have dropped out when you pushed them open! Oh, Scamper – did you get lonely without me? Didn't you *know* I'd gone for a ride on Fred's pony? Silly dog – you only had to wait a little while!'

'You shouldn't really have gone off on the pony,' said his mother. 'Still – all's well that ends well. Now, hadn't you better go back to your job? See – here is an old bag of mine. Put the money into it – and *guard it yourself*.'

Peter raced back to the vicarage, feeling most relieved, Scamper at his heels. How glad the others were to see him and hear what had happened!

'Good old Scamper,' said Janet, patting him. 'You went to find Peter, didn't you? And you took the money with you because you were guarding it. You're a very, very good dog. Come and have an ice-cream!'

'Wuff!' said Scamper, pleased, and off he went with Janet, leaving the others to sell the wooden rings and balls to customers at the hoopla-stall and the coconut-shy.

And, as you can guess, EVERY ONE of the Secret Seven kept their eyes on the money after that – and when all the stalls counted out their takings, the money brought in by the Secret Seven was more than that taken at any other stall. How very proud they felt!

'Well done, you Seven,' said Mrs James. 'We really couldn't have done without you!'

'WUFF!' said Scamper at once – and, as Janet said, that meant, 'And you CERTAINLY couldn't have done without ME!'

Where are the Secret Seven?

'Wuff!' said Scamper, as he saw Peter and Janet getting out their bicycles. 'Wuff!'

'No – you can't come with us today', said Peter. 'Sorry, Scamper, but we're going too fast for you. All the seven of us are going to explore that old ruined house on the side of Hallows Hill. You stay here like a good dog.'

Scamper put his tail down and whined. It was too bad of the Seven to go off without him. Peter and Janet got on their bicycles and away they went to join the others, who were waiting for them at the top of the lane.

'Hallo, Barbara, hallo, Pam!' cried Janet, as she saw the other two girls who belonged to the Secret Seven.

'Hallo, Colin and George!' shouted Peter. 'Where's Jack? Oh, there you are, Jack. Are we all ready – well, off we go to Hallows Hill!'

Away they went, shouting and laughing to one another. It was fun to be together again on a fine Saturday morning – no school, no work to do – just a lovely day, a picnic and a little exploration of a strange old place!

Hallows Hill wasn't really very far if you went across the fields – but much longer by the road. The sun shone down hotly, and the Seven began to pant as they came to the hill on which stood the strange old house.

'There it is!' said Colin. 'It's awfully old – and there are strange stories about it. Especially one about a dog.'

'About a dog? Why, what story is there?' asked Pam. 'Tell it to us!'

They had to get off their bicycles to walk up the steep path, and Colin told them the odd story.

'Well, it's said that once a dog lived there till he was very, very old – and one day his master fell down the stone stairs and couldn't move – and the dog barked all day and night for help. And now it's said that he can still be heard barking at certain times, though the old house is ruined and empty.'

'Poor old dog,' said Janet. 'I'm sure Scamper would do the same if anything happened to *us*. He'd bark the place down – and *his* bark would go echoing down the years too! It's such a very loud one!'

Everyone laughed. Jack pointed to an old stone tower which had just come into sight round a corner. 'Look, there's the old place,' he said. 'It's a pity it's fallen into ruins – it must have been a lovely house once.'

Jackdaws flew round the old house, and perched on the broken tower. 'We shall be able to see their nests,' said Peter. 'They build them of twigs and I bet the tower is full of old nests made of twigs and sticks!'

They were soon in the old house. It was bigger than they had imagined, and they wandered from room to room, looking all round. It was quite empty of furniture, of course – but the old stoves were still in the kitchen, and the old pump there still worked! Colin and Jack worked the handle up and down – and water spouted into the cracked old sink!

'There are still some broken dishes in the larder!' called Janet, opening a great door. 'My word – what a larder! It's as big as our sitting-room at home!'

'And come and look here!' shouted Jack. 'There's an *enormous* room here – it must have been a ballroom, I should think. See, there are still mirrors all round the walls.'

They stood and looked round the silent, dusty, cobwebby room in wonder. They imagined it lighted with hundreds of candles, the floor gleaming and polished, and beautifully dressed people dancing all night through in years gone by.

Then Colin suddenly spotted something on the floor. 'Look – cigarette ends!' he said. 'Someone besides ourselves comes here! There's a newspaper too – and dead matches – and greasy paper.'

'For sandwiches, I expect,' said Peter. 'Why didn't they clear up their litter?'

'I say – come and look *here!*' called Janet, from a great old chimney-place. 'If you look up this chimney you can see the blue sky ever so far up, like a little blue patch. There aren't any jackdaw nests here!'

'Why – it's big enough to stand up in!' said Pam, in wonder, standing in the fire-place, with her head up the enormous chimney-opening. 'They could have roasted a bullock here!'

They all examined the chimney-place and then George gave a shout. 'There are steps at the side here – I bet they lead into an old hiding-place. I'm going up to see!' And up he went and stumbled into a dark little room hollowed out of the great chimney stack. He felt in his pocket for his torch, and switched it on. He stared in surprise at what he saw!

'Peter! Something's hidden in here. There are lots of boxes and . . .'

But suddenly a loud voice cut across what he was shouting. 'Hey! What are you kids doing here? Come out of that chimney-place, quick now!'

George stumbled down the steps from the little hidden room and joined the others, astonished. A tall man was standing on the hearth, looking very angry.

'I say,' began George, 'what are those boxes up in that . . .'

'Oh – so you've seen those, have you?' said the man. 'Well, that settles it! I'll have to keep you prisoner here till I've got them away. Get into that big larder over there – all of you – quick, or I'll box your ears!'

Very scared now, the Seven ran to the great larder. The enormous door was slammed on them, and they heard the key turned in the lock.

'You'll come to no harm,' called the man, 'but there you'll stay till me and my pals have taken our stuff away. If kids come snooping round they have to take what's coming to them – it serves you right!'

Pam began to cry, and Janet and Barbara looked scared. 'Cheer up!' said Peter. 'We've discovered some kind of hiding-place for stolen goods, I expect – and that man has shut us up to be out of the way. I'm afraid we'll be here all night, though – that fellow's friends wouldn't risk removing boxes in full daylight!'

It was very boring in the great larder. A small barred window let in air, and an enormous draught blew under the door. There was a space of about two inches there, and the wind blew under it. Pam felt her feet growing colder and colder.

'I'm going to get up on this shelf out of the draught', she said. 'My feet are frozen! Oh Peter – shall we really have to say here all night?'

'Well, I don't see how we can get out', said Peter. 'I only wish we could! I'd like to tell the police about this, before those boxes are removed – but we can't tell anybody anything while we're locked up here! George – come and try and break down the door with me – and you too, Colin and Jack.'

But although they threw themselves against the door time and time again, it would not budge. The lock was old but good. In the end they all clambered up on the

larder shelves to get out of the draught that blew under the space below the door.

Time went on. They ate all the food they had brought. They played guessing games and asked each other riddles – but oh dear, how boring it was to be shut up for hours like this!

And then Pam lifted her head, and listened, looking rather scared. 'Listen!' she said.

'What is it?' said Colin. 'Oh that – it's only a dog barking somewhere.'

'I know – but – but don't you remember the tale you told us about the dog of long ago?' said Pam. 'Do you think it might be him? There can't be any dogs near here – it's such a lonely place!'

But before they had time to be frightened the barking came much nearer – and a brown nose snuffled suddenly under the larder door!

'It's SCAMPER!' yelled Peter, in delight. 'Scamper – you've tracked us here – even though we were on our bicycles! Oh, good dog, good dog!'

'Wuff, wuff, wuff!' said Scamper, trying to paw under the larder door. Janet suddenly had a wonderful idea.

'Peter! You could get hold of Scamper's collar under the door – there's such a big space there. And you could tie a note on it and send him home with it to Daddy! Oh, quick, quick!'

What a marvellous idea! Peter soon carried it out. He scribbled a note on a page in his diary, tore it out, borrowed a piece of string from Jack, and tied it firmly to Scamper's collar, pulling it as far under the door as he could. Scamper was surprised to have his collar grabbed

at, but, as usual, very willing to help the Seven! Away he
went when Peter commanded him: 'Home, now! Home!
Take the note to Daddy!'

'If only Daddy and the police get here in time!' said
Janet. 'It will soon be dark now! Well – we must wait
patiently!'

But they didn't have to wait very long! Scamper raced
home by the short cut through the fields this time, and
soon delivered the note to Peter's astonished father – and
in no time at all he had got out his car, collected two
policemen and was speeding up the hill to the old house!

What an excitement! The larder door was opened, and
the children poured out, eagerly telling their story! Colin
showed where the boxes were hidden, and the two
policemen whistled when they saw them.

'They're full of priceless things stolen from the museum
in the next town!' said one. 'Well – we'll wait here for the
fellow who locked you in – and see who he and his friends
are. You kids must go home with your father. You can't
be mixed up in this – there may be some trouble!'

'*Why* can't we stay?' said Peter, indignantly. But it was
no good – home they all had to go, hungry and tired, but
very excited. To think they had had such an adventure on
a Saturday morning!

'The men will be caught, and the goods taken back to
the Museum,' said Peter's father, as he drove the children
home. 'Well, I congratulate the Seven – but I'm even
more pleased with Somebody else!'

'Yes – Scamper!' cried everyone – and what a lot of
pats he got. Good old Scamper! He really deserves the
enormous bone he's going to get!

Hurry, Secret Seven, hurry!

THE SECRET Seven had been out together for a picnic. Scamper was with them, his tail wagging happily. He loved being alone with Peter and Janet – but it was even better to be with the whole of the Seven! There was always somebody fussing him then, patting him, or talking to him.

'Well, I must say the baskets weigh a lot lighter coming *home* from a picnic than *going* to one!' said Janet, swinging hers to and fro. 'Oooh, sorry, Colin – I didn't know you were just behind me.'

'You'd better give that basket to Scamper to carry,' said Colin. 'That's three times you've banged me with it.'

'Shall we go home through the fields or through the town?' said Peter.

'Through the town!' said everyone. They were all thinking the same thing – what about a call at the ice-cream shop?

So they went back through the town. It was market-day and the streets were full. People rushed about here and there, carrying parcels, calling to one another, and cars had to go very slowly indeed because there were so many people walking in the road.

A man came down the street, cycling quickly. He rang his bell as if he were in a great hurry, and people tried to get out of the way. Peter just skipped to one side in time as the man cycled past. He turned to stare after him indignantly. 'He almost knocked me over,' began Peter, and then stopped. Even as he spoke, something had happened.

CRASH! The man on the bicycle had bumped into a car and had been flung off into the road. A woman gave a loud scream and people hurried up at once.

The children ran to see what had happened. The man lay there, half-dazed, his head badly bruised, and his cheek cut. A policeman came up.

'He was going so *fast*,' said a woman near by. 'He kept shouting to people to get out of the way. He was in an awful hurry and didn't seem to see that car.'

The man tried to speak and the policeman bent down. He listened hard and looked puzzled. 'He keeps saying "Gate,"' he said. 'Is that his name? Does anyone know?'

More people crowded up and the policeman began to send them off. 'Now, now – move away,' he said. 'Ah, here's a doctor. *Will* you move away, you kids? Give the poor fellow a chance.'

The Secret Seven moved off with all the other children who had crowded round. 'I'll never ride *my* bicycle fast,' said Barbara. 'I never will, now I've seen how suddenly accidents can happen.'

'Who was the man? Do you know?' asked Peter.

'I've never seen him before,' said Pam.

'Well, I seem to know his face,' said George, puzzled. 'Yes, I know I do. But I just can't think *who* he is.'

'*I* think I've seen him before, too,' said Jack, frowning. 'I've watched him doing something. What on earth can it be?'

'Oh, never mind,' said Pam. 'What does it matter? He's in safe hands now, with a policeman there and a doctor.'

'I just *can't* remember,' said George. 'It's no good. I sort of feel he's something to do with the railway. He's not one of the porters, is he?'

'No,' said Jack, who knew all the porters because he so often went to meet his father off the train. 'He's not a porter – he's not the ticket-clerk either, or the station-master. All the same, I can't help thinking you're right – he *is* something to do with the railway.'

'Oh, stop bothering about it,' said Pam. 'I want to forget the accident. It was horrid.'

They walked along, swinging their baskets and bags, Peter and Colin arguing about football, and the three girls listening. Suddenly George interrupted.

'I know! I've remembered who that man is!' he said. 'And we're right – he *is* something to do with the railway.'

'Is his name Gate?' asked Janet.

'No,' said George. '"Gate" is part of his work, though. He's the man who opens and shuts the gate at the railway-crossing! You know – we've often watched him coming out of his little cottage and swing the big gates open, one after the other – and then shutting them over the line when the train has passed.'

'Oh *yes* – of course! You're right,' said Jack. 'It's Mr Williams, the level-crossing man!'

'I say – I hope there's someone at his cottage who will

open the gates for the next train!' said Peter, stopping suddenly. 'That's why he was in such a hurry, I expect. He wanted to get back in time to open the gates.'

'The six-fifteen is due soon,' said Colin. 'My father's on it!'

'Let's go back quickly and tell the policeman!' said Janet, suddenly feeling scared at the thought of a train racing along the lines and crashing into closed crossing-gates.

'No time,' said Peter, looking at his watch. Then, like a good leader, he made up his mind quickly. 'This may be serious,' he said. 'If there's no one at Williams' cottage to open the gates for the next train, there'll certainly be a smash. Even if the train doesn't rock off the lines, those big gates will be smashed to pieces. Buck up – we'll run to the cottage and find out if anyone is there.'

The seven children, with Scamper racing behind barking excitedly, ran down the road and round the corner. Down the next road and up a little hill and down again – and there, some way in front of them, stretched the railway-line.

'Buck up!' panted Peter. 'We're nearly there. We've still got a few minutes before the train is due.'

Peter reached the cottage first. It stood close beside the level-crossing, a pretty little place with a tiny garden of its own. Peter yelled as he ran up to it.

'Is there anyone at home! I say – is there anyone in?'

He banged at the door and then rang the bell beside it. Nobody answered. Nobody came. Then Colin ran to the window and looked inside.

'ANYONE IN?' he shouted at the top of his voice. He turned round. 'The place is empty!' he said. 'That's why Williams was biking so fast to get back. He hadn't left anyone to see to the gates!'

'And that's why he kept saying "Gate! Gate!"' said Janet. 'What *are* we to do?'

'Open the gates ourselves, of course,' said Peter, trying to be as calm as possible. He could see that the three girls were getting excited and alarmed. That would never do. Everyone must keep calm, everyone must help. Those gates were very, very heavy!

Colin looked round to see if anyone was near who could help them. A strong man would be most welcome! But not a soul was there except a small girl, who stared at them solemnly all the time.

'George, Janet! Come with me to the nearest gate and help me to open it!' shouted Peter. 'Jack, you go to the other one with Pam and Barbara and Colin. And for goodness' sake make haste! The train's due in about a minute!'

'We must all look out for it!' shouted Colin. 'It will be down on us at top speed before we know where we are!'

Soon all seven children were straining hard at the heavy gates. A great bolt had to be lifted from its hole in the ground first, and then an iron ring undone at the top of the post. It held the gate closed, and only when it was lifted back from the post would the gate open.

'I can hear the train!' yelled Janet, who had very sharp ears. 'And the lines are beginning to tremble. Hurry, hurry!'

Colin, with three people to help him, managed to open his gate first and swing it slowly across the line and back,

so that the way was clear. But Peter's bolt was stiff and took a good deal of easing up.

'The train's coming!' screamed Pam. 'The train's coming! Get away, Peter, get away!'

Yes – the train was certainly coming. It whistled as it came roaring along, and when Peter looked up he could see it tearing down the line towards them.

With a last heave, he got the bolt out of its hole. Then, with all the others now helping, he swung the gate back as quickly as he could. Pam screamed again as the engine raced past her, making quite a wind. A surprised driver looked out of the cab at the children on the line beside him. Then the long row of swaying carriages came rumbling past, making a truly enormous noise.

In a few moments the train was gone, racing away down the line, growing smaller and smaller every minute. Soon it would draw in at the station a mile away, and Colin's father would fold his evening paper and get out.

'I wonder if Dad saw me?' said Colin as the train raced away.

'I feel rather faint,' said Barbara suddenly, and sat down against one of the gates. 'Oh dear – how silly.'

'It's just the excitement,' said Peter, whose heart was thumping so hard in his chest that he found it quite difficult to speak. 'My word, we didn't have much time. But we just did it!'

A shout came to their ears, and they turned. It was the policeman on a bicycle, with two or three men behind in a car.

'Hey – what are you doing on the lines, you children? Did anything happen to the gates?'

'No. We managed to open them for the train,' shouted back Peter.

'Well, I'm blessed,' said the policeman, getting off his bicycle as the three men jumped out of their car.

'Did you remember the gates when you found out who that man was who was knocked down?' asked Peter.

'Yes – the fellow managed to tell us at last,' said the policeman. 'I shot off at once – and these men came in their car as soon as they could. My word – when I saw the train racing by, I thought everything was up! I listened for the gates to be smashed – but no, the train just raced by as usual.'

'You mean to say you kids opened them?' said one of the other men. 'How did you think of such a thing?'

'We remembered who that man was – Mr Williams, the crossing-gates man,' said George. 'Then we thought of the gates – and the train that was due – and we ran like hares to open them.'

'We only *just* managed it,' said Jack. 'Whew – I'm dripping wet! They *were* heavy, those gates!'

'I'm melting, too!' said Barbara, who was still sitting down, but already looking a little better.

'Who *are* you children?' said another man, a big, burly fellow, looking at them hard. 'You seem a jolly good bunch of kids, I must say! You've probably saved a lot of damage, you know.'

'We're the Secret Seven,' said Peter proudly, and tapped his badge. 'Ready to do any job of work, at any time!'

'So I see,' said the man. 'Well, I'm a railway official, so you can take it from me that you've saved us pounds and pounds of damage by opening those gates – besides possibly a nasty accident. The train *might* have swerved off the rails when it hit the gates.'

'I'm jolly glad it didn't,' said Colin. 'My father's on that train! Wait till I tell him our tale tonight!'

'Well, before you do that, I'd like you to do something else for me, if you will,' said the big man, and winked at his two companions.

'What's that?' asked Peter, with visions of another exciting bit of work to do.

'Help me to eat a few ice-creams!' said the man. 'You look so hot – you ought to cool down. And that would be a good way of doing it – don't you think so?'

'Oooh yes!' said everyone, and Barbara stood up at once. She felt quite prepared to eat at least three ice-creams if this man offered them!

The two men with him went to swing the gates back across the lines again, so that people might pass over on foot or in cars. The big man got into his car, and told the children to follow him to the ice-cream shop just down the road.

Soon they were all sitting together, with such enormous ice-creams that they really couldn't believe their eyes.

'This is the biggest ice-cream I've ever had in my life,' said Peter.

'You deserve it, old son,' said the big man, who was eating an ice-cream, too. 'How in the world did you open those gates in time! You had only a few minutes to race away from Williams, get down to the crossing, and swing back those heavy gates. I don't know *how* you did it!'

'Yes – you're right,' said Peter, thinking about it. '*I* don't quite know how we did it, either. But the thing is – we *did* it!'

Well that's really all that matters, Secret Seven. You saw what had to be done – and YOU DID IT!